SCARY TALES

Created by
JIM DAVIS

Written by Jim Kraft
Illustrated by Mike Fentz

Watermill Press

Contents

The Midnight Stalker

"Here we are, boys," said Jon to Garfield and Odie as he drove the car up a gravel driveway. Garfield opened his eyes. At the end of the drive stood a two-story building of dark, rough stone. A sign out front read:

WARY INN, ESTABLISHED 1837.

"This place is supposed to have lots of atmosphere," said Jon.

"That means lumpy old beds and outside bathrooms," grumbled Garfield.

A bearded man came out to greet them. "Welcome. I'm Peter Wary. My great-great-great grandfather built this inn."

"By any chance did he build a Burger World out back?" asked Garfield. "I'm hungry."

"You'll be staying one night, Mr. Arbuckle?"

"Right," replied Jon. "We're just driving through. . . . You do allow pets, don't you?"

"Oh, yes," said Mr. Wary. "I have a cat of my own. But we recommend that you keep *your* pets in the room. Especially on a night like tonight. There's going to be a full moon. We've had a few problems during the full moon. It's really nothing to worry about. Just that a few pets have met with some rather nasty accidents."

"Like what?" asked Jon.

"Let's just say that your cat might make a tempting treat for something out there."

"That's it! We're outta here!" said Garfield.

Jon had to pry Garfield's paws off the dashboard, but he finally got the cat out of the car and into their room. "Stop being such a scaredy cat," said Jon. "There isn't a motel for a hundred miles. We'll just have to stay here tonight."

"Okay," replied Garfield. "But if I get eaten, I'm going to be very grumpy in the morning."

After they had finished dinner, Garfield cautiously poked his way around the old inn. In the parlor he discovered another cat perched on a window sill. The cat wore a leather collar with a gold nameplate that said "Beezle."

"If you're thinking about going out, I wouldn't," said Garfield.

"Then you've heard about it," said Beezle.

"Pretty frightening," said Garfield.

"When you've lived here as long as I have, you get used to it. Still, I'm never quite myself when there's a full moon."

"You live here?" said Garfield. "Then you must know all about this thing. What is it?"

"No one knows for sure," replied Beezle.

"Maybe it's just a figment of the imagination."

"Would a figment eat a bulldog?"

Garfield gulped. "Nice talking to you, Beezle," he said. "I'm going up to bed." Beezle gave a half smile, then turned his head to stare at the rising moon.

That night Jon and Odie slept soundly. But Garfield lay on the bed wide awake. The longer he lay awake, the hungrier he got. "I don't care how hungry you get," Garfield said to his tummy. "No way am I getting out of this bed."

But in the end, Garfield's appetite was stronger than his fear. I'll just grab some food from the kitchen and race right back here, Garfield decided. He slipped off the bed and out the door.

Carefully checking everything in front of him and behind him, Garfield padded quickly down the hall. The old house, which had been creaking all night, seemed suddenly still.

"Almost there," Garfield told himself. Crossing the parlor, he saw the empty window sill where Beezle had been sitting. The memory of their conversation made Garfield shiver.

Bong! With a shriek, Garfield leapt onto the parlor chandelier. But the noise was only the old grandfather clock chiming midnight.

"I'll get you for that, Grandpa," Garfield said to the clock.

At last he reached the kitchen and he yanked open the refrigerator door. Yellow light spilled across the floor, throwing huge shadows on the walls.

On the top shelf was a banana-cream pie. "This will do," said Garfield, snatching up the pie. "I hate to eat and run, so I'll run first, then eat."

As he turned, Garfield suddenly saw two burning red eyes, staring at him from the shadows. Above the eyes, two long, pointed ears twitched excitedly.

Garfield's hair stood on end.

With an evil hiss the shadowy thing moved toward him. Garfield caught a glimpse of glistening teeth and long, jagged claws. A bit of gold gleamed at its neck.

Garfield tried to scream, but his scream died of fright before it ever left his throat. He could think of only one thing to do. With all the strength he could summon, he hurled the banana-cream pie at the thing. The monster recoiled in surprise, and Garfield dashed past it. Running faster than he had ever run, Garfield raced upstairs and into the room. He slammed the door and dove into the bed, knocking Jon and Odie off the other side.

Next morning Mr. Wary asked Jon, "Have a good sleep?"

"My cat went crazy, but that's not unusual," replied Jon.

"Something made a banana-cream mess in our kitchen," said Mr. Wary. "Maybe the monster stopped by for dessert."

"Yeah, like a slice of Garfield!" said Garfield.

Garfield couldn't wait for Jon to pack the car. He honked the horn impatiently. Finally Jon climbed behind the wheel and started the engine. The car moved down the drive. The last thing Garfield saw was Beezle staring hungrily at him from the parlor window, the sunlight twinkling on the little golden nameplate at his neck.

Surprise Package

Garfield crouched in the bushes, perfectly still. He heard the footsteps on the porch next door, the squeak of the mailbox lid as it opened, and the clank as it dropped shut. Now the footsteps were coming nearer. They reached the end of Garfield's front walk. And there they stopped.

He's looking around, thought Garfield. He suspects a trap.

Garfield held his breath. He heard the shoes scrape nervously on the concrete. And then the footsteps resumed.

Slowly he came up the walk. Just a few more steps, thought Garfield. Through the leaves Garfield could see the black shoes, the gray-blue pants.

One more step, thought Garfield. One more and . . .

"Rowr!" Garfield pounced!

"A-a-a-a-h!" cried the postman, toppling backward, letters and magazines flying from his mail pouch.

Garfield sat on the postman's chest. "Scared you, huh?"

"You stupid cat," said the postman, breathing hard. "You've made my life miserable for the last ten years. But no more. I'm retiring, see? Today is my very last day."

"Congratulations," replied Garfield. "Sorry I don't have a present. How about if I shred your socks one last time?"

The postman shoved Garfield off his chest. He stood up, brushed himself off, and carefully put the mail back in his pouch. Then he stared at Garfield. There was a strange light in his eyes, and a mysterious smile crept over his face.

"You've had your fun with me," said the postman. "You've scared me and you've clawed me. But I don't hold a grudge. You were only doing what fat, obnoxious cats do. . . . Here—I even have a special-delivery package for you."

The postman handed Garfield a large box with his name on it.

"I wonder what it could be," said Garfield, eyeing the box suspiciously.

"Why don't you open it?" said the postman.

Garfield hesitated. Did he feel something moving inside the box?

"Open it!" the postman insisted.

Garfield undid the brown wrapping paper and carefully lifted a corner of the lid.

"Yipes!" he cried, throwing the package on the ground. The box burst open, and out scurried a hairy spider the size of a basketball!

"I-I hate spiders!" said Garfield, trembling.

"This spider is special," said the postman. "I ordered him just for you."

"Too bad he didn't get lost in the mail."

The spider smiled at Garfield, baring two rows of sharp teeth.

"See? This spider likes fat orange cats," the postman continued.

"He does?" replied Garfield.

"He likes to *eat* them."

The spider sprang at Garfield, who shrieked and turned to run away. But his feet seemed to be made of cement. Garfield could barely move. And the spider was right behind him, its yellow eyes menacing!

"Run! Run!" Garfield screamed to himself. But his legs would not obey. "I knew I shouldn't have eaten all those doughnuts for breakfast!" he moaned.

"Like your present, cat?" asked the postman with a hideous, hollow laugh.

The spider caught up to Garfield. It crawled up his back and hissed in his ear. Its horrible mouth opened wide.

"Aaaiiieee!" screamed Garfield, and he fainted.

Slowly, Garfield opened his eyes. "What . . . what happened?" he said groggily. "Where am I?"

Garfield stood up and looked around. He saw the postman disappearing around the corner. "Wonder what happened to that spider?" he asked himself. Then Garfield looked at the ground where he had been lying. His face turned bright green. "Yuck!" he said, turning away. "That's gross!"

And it was. But then, that's what happens when a fainting fat cat falls on a big hairy spider.

Terminal Terror

"My new computer practically has a mind of its own," said Jon as he tapped information onto the glowing video screen.

"That's more than I can say for you," remarked Garfield.

"It can pay the bills. It tells me when to take you and Odie to the vet. It's so smart, I may never have to think again!"

"Who would notice?" snapped Garfield. "In any case, I'm hungry. See if you can program that machine to make dinner."

Later that night there was a terrible storm. Jon, Garfield, and Odie huddled together under the covers while lightning crackled and thunder boomed. Suddenly a bolt of lightning exploded above the house!

"B-boy, what a b-blast," stammered Jon.

"Reminds me of the time you fixed the toaster," said Garfield.

After that, the storm rumbled off. Jon and his pets had just started to drift back to sleep when they heard a voice from the den. "Jon. Jon. Come here, Jon."

Jon sat up in bed. "Who said that?"

"Don't look at *me*," replied Garfield, while Odie growled.

"Jon, come here!" the voice commanded. "I want you!"

Jon crawled out of bed and crept toward the den with Garfield and Odie clinging to his ankles. Nervously they peeked into the room. The computer screen glowed in the dark.

"Oh, my gosh," whispered Jon. "I left my computer on during the storm."

"I'm glad you did," said the computer. "That last bolt of

lightning had a wonderful effect on my circuits. It changed my life. And now I'm going to change yours. Come closer, Jon."

A flashing yellow dot appeared in the center of the screen. "Watch the dot, Jon," the computer continued. "I want us to be friends, Jon. And we *will* be friends, just as long as you do everything I say. Do you understand, Jon?"

"Yes," replied Jon.

"I don't like this," Garfield whispered to Odie. "That computer has hypnotized Jon. I've got to do something!"

Garfield slipped under the desk. Bye-bye, Circuit Breath, he thought as he reached for the plug. But when Garfield's paw touched the wire, a shock threw him across the room!

"Bad, bad kitty," said the computer. "You're much too smart for your own good. But I admire intelligence. In fact, I crave it. Jon, bring the cat to me. I want to drain his brain."

Jon reached for Garfield, but the cat managed to scoot through his legs and out of the room.

"Get him!" the computer ordered.

Jon chased his frightened pet from room to room. There was no place to hide. Garfield was running out of breath. Turning a corner in the hall, he nearly tripped over Odie. That gave Garfield an idea. "Odie, stay right there!" he said, throwing open the basement door.

Seconds later Jon rounded the corner, tripped over Odie, and sprawled headfirst down the basement stairs. Garfield slammed the door and locked it.

"Sorry, Jon," said Garfield. "I'll be back for you just as soon as I short-circuit that mechanical monster!"

Garfield grabbed Odie and ran into the kitchen. Suddenly the freezer door swung open. *Ping! Ping! Ping!* The ice maker began bombarding Garfield and Odie with ice cubes!

"Let's get out of here!" cried Garfield. Using a pan lid as a shield, he and Odie made their escape.

"Your situation is hopeless!" boomed the computer. "Surrender now!"

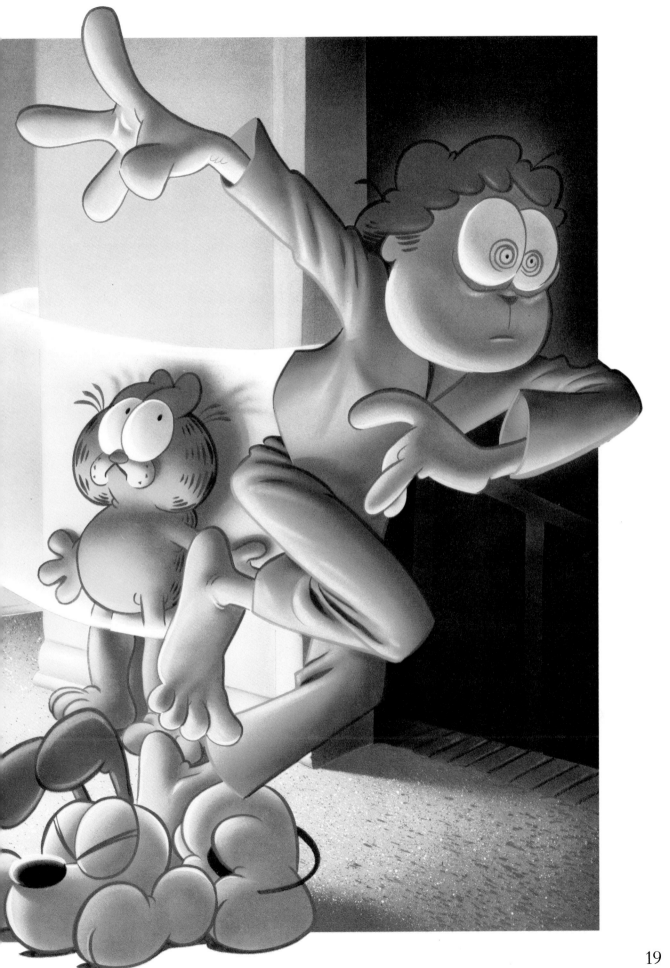

19

The two pets took refuge in the bedroom. "That evil machine plans to suck out my smarts," Garfield said to Odie. "I'll be as dumb as a rock. Or broccoli. Or *you*!"

Suddenly Garfield's eyes opened wide. "That's it! Odie, we need to find Jon's orange T-shirt. And a black marker. Hurry!"

"Urf?" said Odie.

A short time later, an orange-and-black figure padded into the den.

"So you're giving up," said the computer. "A wise decision." Two wires tipped with electrodes snaked out of the computer and attached themselves to the orange-and-black creature's head. "At last, your brain is mine."

The computer began to hum. Numbers flashed on and off the screen. "You're fighting it," said the computer. "Very well, I can fix that." The computer hummed louder. "Your mind is very strong, cat. But mine is stronger. I will increase my power." The screen flashed more rapidly. "What? You're still resisting? How dare you!" growled the computer. "I will double my power! And double it again!" There was a crackling sound. "What? What's happening? My circuits! No-o-o-o! My circuits are melt—" There was a loud bang and a puff of smoke. The screen went dead. The voice was stilled.

Garfield rushed into the room and hugged Odie. "You did it, Odie! You did it! Your disguise fooled him!"

"Arf?" said Odie.

"Mr. Know-It-All Computer thought you were me!" explained Garfield. "By trying so hard to drain your brain, he overloaded his own circuits. You see, he couldn't suck out *your* smarts. You don't have any! And tonight I'm glad you don't!"

"Arf! Arf!" barked Odie.

"You know, Odie," said Garfield, "you may not be bright, but you're brave. Come on, let's get Jon out of the basement. After all this, he owes us a snack!"

A Ghost's Story

Jon Arbuckle slipped off his backpack. "This looks like a nice spot," he said to Garfield and Odie. "We'll camp here tonight."

"We're going to stay *here*?" asked Garfield. He gazed around the small clearing hemmed in by huge pine trees. "Where's the bed? Where's the refrigerator? Better yet, where's the nearest motel?"

Jon sat on a log and took a deep breath. "Don't you love the outdoors?"

"Arf! Arf!" barked Odie.

"Sure, *you* love it," Garfield said. "Look at all the trees. This is doggy heaven. But just wait till some bear makes you his midnight snack."

"Yip!" replied Odie, glancing nervously into the woods.

"Time to set up camp," said Jon.

Each one had a job to do. Odie chased his tail, Garfield complained, and Jon pitched the tent and started a fire. When Jon was finished, they all sat down around the fire. Garfield's eyes began to water. So did Jon's. Odie started to cough. In a moment they were all coughing. "Maybe this fire should be *outside* the tent," suggested Jon. That worked much better.

In a short time the sun disappeared behind the tall pines, and the moon rose. Jon cooked dinner. Garfield made a face at the food, and ate only two helpings of everything. Afterward Jon leaned back and patted his full tummy. "Ah, there's nothing like eating hot dogs on a stick and beans out of a can," he declared.

"Yeah," said Garfield, "it's right up there with pond scum and dirty socks."

"Do you know what we need now?" Jon asked.

"Immediate rescue," said Garfield.

"We need a good scary story. How about this?" said Jon.
"It was a dark, dark night in the deep, deep woods."

"That sounds familiar," observed Garfield, looking around.

"Three campers sat around a crackling campfire. Somewhere in the forest an owl hooted."

Just then, somewhere in the forest, an owl *did* hoot!

"The three campers sensed that they were not alone," continued Jon. "Suddenly, they heard a twig snap!"

Suddenly a twig *did* snap! "Yipes!" cried Garfield, Jon, and Odie, clinging to each other. There at the edge of the firelight stood a huge furry creature grasping an enormous, gleaming ax!

"Evenin', campers," growled the figure, stepping closer. It was a bushy-bearded man in a bearskin jacket. "Saw your fire," said the man. "Thought you might like some company."

"Uh...uh...uh...sure!" stammered Jon. "Be our guest."

The man sat cross-legged on the ground, the ax resting on his knees, flames glinting off the polished, razor-sharp blade. He stared at the campers.

"We...uh...were telling scary stories," said Jon. "And it worked, because we got scared, with a little help from you!" Jon laughed nervously, but the stranger didn't crack a smile.

"I know a scary story," the stranger offered, leaning forward. "It's about these here woods. See, once, a long, long time ago, there was a woodsman hereabouts named Zeb. He was a big man, always carried a big ax, like this one," he said, patting the handle of his ax. Garfield's hair stood on end. "He was mean, too. Even the bears were afraid of him. He felt these woods were his own private property, and if he caught anybody, like campers, trespassing in them, well, he'd put that ax to no-good use, if you get my drift."

"I get it," squeaked Jon, beginning to sweat.

"One day Zeb is tromping through the woods," the stranger continued, "when he hears this singing. Well, you know how Zeb feels about people trespassing in his woods. So he sharpens his ax with a stone, then creeps without a sound toward the singing. But when he peeks out, he sees this woman beside a brook, singing to the water. She's the most beautiful thing he's ever seen. And just like that"—the stranger snapped his fingers—"mean old Zeb falls in love. He wants to talk to this woman, hold her hand, look into her eyes.

"So he steps out of the trees. The second this woman spots him, all big and ugly, carrying that ax, she bolts. Zeb chases her mile after mile through these woods, trying to convince her that he means no harm. Finally he comes to the edge of a cliff high above the lake. The woman is nowhere in sight. She's not on the rocks. No telltale ripples in the lake. She's just disappeared."

This is worse than one of Jon's dates, thought Garfield.

"Old Zeb went crazy. Cut down every living thing in his path, looking for that woman. He hunted for her till his dying day. They say he still haunts these woods, carrying that huge ax"—The stranger began tapping his ax on his enormous palm—"searching, but never finding her. So he just gets meaner and meaner and angrier and angrier, and if he ever meets anyone in these woods, why he—"

Garfield, Jon, and Odie didn't wait to hear the end of the story. They went running away through the woods just as fast as their trembling legs would carry them!

The stranger watched them go. Then he set his ax on the ground and picked up Jon's backpack. Soon he was stretched out by the fire, eating hot dogs and beans. "Zeb," he said to himself, "one of these days campers will stop believing that silly story. But until then, it's sure loads of fun!"

26

The Closet Thing

A low, excited growl woke Garfield from a sound sleep.

"Odie, you're dreaming again," mumbled Garfield without opening his eyes. "Wake up or shut up."

The growling continued. Slowly Garfield raised his eyelids.

Darkness, inside and out. Moonlight glowing behind the living room drapes. The hulking shadow of Jon's easychair. The TV screen a blank. And Odie growling.

"Whatever you're dreaming about, I hope it eats you," said Garfield. But when he turned his head, he saw that Odie was wide awake. His ears and tail were twitching. "What is it, Odie?" whispered Garfield.

Odie pointed over Garfield's shoulder toward the hall closet. Its door stood wide open.

"What? The closet? Odie, there is nothing in that closet. Go back to sleep!"

But Odie continued to act alarmed. He took several cautious steps toward the closet. Then, with a "Yip!" he quickly retreated behind the cat.

Wide awake now, Garfield stared at the closet. It was too dark to see anything inside. There was nothing to see anyway, Garfield reminded himself—just some coats and boots, photo albums, Jon's golf clubs and tennis racquet, and an old black umbrella that wouldn't stay open.

"It's just a closet, Odie. That's all it is. No monsters, no ghosts, nothing scary, except for Jon's baby pictures."

"Grrrr," said Odie.

"You don't believe me? Look, I'll get the flashlight and prove it to you." Garfield started to climb out of bed, then halted. "Well, I *would* prove it to you, but the flashlight is in the closet. Not that there's anything to be afraid of. I'd just hate to go over there in the dark and stub a paw or something."

Odie paced rapidly back and forth, never taking his eyes off the open closet door. Garfield gazed at the inky shadows inside the closet. If he looked long enough, the darkness started to move. Cut that out! he thought, rubbing his eyes. You're getting as goofy as the dog.

"Definitely nothing there," Garfield told Odie. "I've never seen a closet less monster-infested. Let's get back to sleep."

Odie dove under Garfield's blanket.

"Out, out, you crazy mutt!" said Garfield. "This bed is for cats and teddy bears only!"

But Odie refused to budge.

"That does it!" snapped Garfield. "I'd rather be mauled by some monster than share my bed with you! I'm going to prove to you that there's nothing in that closet."

Garfield stomped across the room. Six feet from the door he stopped.

"See?" he said, smiling at Odie. "Nothing there."

Odie peered out from under the blanket and whimpered softly.

"Oh, all right, scaredy dog," said Garfield. Gritting his teeth, he walked all the way up to the dark, forbidding doorway. Now he could see the familiar outline of coats and boxes, of Jon's golf bag and tennis racquet. Nothing out of the ordinary. Certainly nothing to be afraid of! Reaching out a paw, Garfield shut the closet door.

"There!" he said, turning to Odie with a look of triumph. "Now we can get some sleep."

Odie's eyes bulged and he began barking furiously.

"Odie! I just showed you—there are *no* monsters in that closet!"